A NEW KIND OF
WILD

BY ZARA
GONZÁLEZ
HOANG

DIAL BOOKS FOR YOUNG READERS

Ren lived in a little white house on the edge of el Yunque.

His days were filled with green
and dirt and rocks and mud. All
the bits of nature and magic a life
lived on the edge of wild offers.

Every day Ren adventured with dragons

and chased unicorns.

He feasted with fairies

and campaigned with kings.

And every night Ren fell asleep to the flickering of fireflies and a chorus of coquís.

It was a place of endless possibility, where anything he imagined became real—at least until bedtime.

This was his home.

COQUÍ
COQUÍ
COQUÍ
COQUÍ
COQUÍ

Until the day it wasn't.

Ren found himself in a brick and cement city.

The friendly sounds of his forest were replaced
by the mechanical creaks and beeps and buzzes
of a place filled with people and progress.

It was too loud and too fast. It made Ren's
head fill up with everything and nothing.
There was no room left for magic,
no room left for wild.

Without his wild, Ren was lonely.

Ava, who lived upstairs, was never lonely. She loved her building and she loved her city.

It was a place of constant change, with people moving through it like an endless parade.

There was always something to see or do, and best of all, there was always someone to share it with.

So when Ava saw Ren, she ran down
to meet him. "I'm Ava," she said.

She asked him who he was and how
he got there. If he had brothers, a
father, a mother. If he liked the city
or why he didn't. She asked him so
many things so quickly, he thought his
head would explode.

When she finally stopped for a breath,
Ren tried to tell her why the city
wasn't for him, but all Ava heard was
a challenge.

Ava pulled him from the stoop and into the busy city.

She led him down colorful streets and sidewalks.

They peeked into alleys,

splashed in hydrants,

and tried to find the rhythm of the streets.

But all Ren saw was gray
and all he heard was the
screeching of brakes and the
honking of horns.

It was nothing like home.

When Ava caught up to Ren, she asked him what was wrong.

"There's no magic here," he said. "No wild. Everything is exactly what it is!"

"You're wrong," Ava said. Hadn't he heard the song of the city, hadn't he seen the color in the streets?

She'd spent all day showing him, how could he not see? If only he would try a little harder, she thought.

But Ren was tired of trying. So he went back inside.

Homesickness swept over him like a wave,
and he felt lonelier than ever.

Outside was a whole new world. One he
didn't belong to. As he stared out the window,
Ren saw Ava skipping across the sidewalk.
She moved through her city like he had moved
through his wild—with an air of possibility
flickering around her.

How did Ava do it? Ren wondered.
Maybe she could show him how.

"Sorry I left," Ren said when he found her. "I just miss home. I've never lived anywhere else and everything is so different here."

"I've only lived in the city," Ava said. "I can't imagine living anywhere else. What is it like?"

So Ren told her about his wild.

About the green and the trees and the rocks and
the mud, and about the magical creatures that
played there. He spun a tale of fairies and fantasy
that he just couldn't see on these drab city blocks.

And finally Ava understood what was missing.

She brought
Ren down to the
basement of their
building.

Showed him how the
shadows could shape-shift
and introduced him to
creatures who lived in the
unlikeliest of places.

Then she took him up.

OUT
OF
ORDER

Past Mr. Borges in apartment 4B, past the empty apartment with the red door, past stacked boxes and peeling wallpaper, all the way to the very top.

She told him that the city had a rhythm and the music it played could be a lullaby or a salsa.

"Listen," she said as she pulled him outside.

The sounds that were so jarring below softened into something almost musical.

With the city spread out before them, Ava showed Ren how bricks could become beautiful.

It was a new kind of wild.

And this time he could see it.

Para mi Papi,
Tus cuentos dan vida a los míos.
Te amo y extraño siempre.

And to anyone who has had to leave
a place they love for somewhere new,
this is for you.

Dial Books for Young Readers
An imprint of Penguin Random House LLC, New York

Copyright © 2020 by Zara González Hoang

Visit us online at penguinrandomhouse.com

Library of Congress Cataloging-in-Publication Data | Names: Hoang, Zara González, author, illustrator.
Title: A new kind of wild / Zara González Hoang. | Description: New York : Dial Books for Young Readers, [2020] |
Summary: "When Ren moves to Ava's city, he feels lost without the green and magic of his home, but not everything in the
city is what meets the eye and Ren discovers that nothing makes you feel at home quite like a friend"—Provided by publisher.
Identifiers: LCCN 2019018643 | ISBN 9780525553892 (hardcover) | Subjects: | CYAC: Moving, Household—Fiction.
| Homesickness—Fiction. | City and town life—Fiction. | Friendship—Fiction. | Classification: LCC PZ7.1.H598 New
2020 | DDC [E]—dc23 | LC record available at https://lccn.loc.gov/2019018643

Printed in China
1 3 5 7 9 10 8 6 4 2

Design by Jennifer Kelly
Text set in Cheltenham BT

The artwork was created with watercolor, colored pencils, and a bit of Photoshop magic.